First published 1988 by
Walker Books Ltd
87 Vauxhall Walk
London SE11 5HJ

Text © 1988 Martin Bax
Illustrations © 1988 Michael Foreman

First printed 1988
Printed and bound by L.E.G.O., Vicenza, Italy

British Library Cataloguing in Publication Data
Bax, Martin
Edmond went far away.
I. Title   II. Foreman, Michael, *1938 –*
823'.914 [J]

ISBN 0-7445-1060-0

EDMOND WENT FAR AWAY

Written by
Martin Bax

Illustrated by
Michael Foreman

WALKER BOOKS
LONDON

Edmond's home

Edmond lived on a farm. The rough track from the road crossed in front of the farm and ran on through the fields down the hill. If you turned one way out of the house you crossed the track to the pond. On the pond there were three white ducks. When Edmond came to the water's edge they turned from whatever they were doing and swam towards him. Sometimes Edmond gave them bread. The ducks and Edmond were good friends.

Across the track from the house there was the big barn with, beside it, the pigsty. In the sty lived a huge, fat sow. Often, she had as many as twelve piglets with her. Just now she had no piglets, but she was very, very fat. She lay on the ground and didn't get up when Edmond came to see her. She opened her eyes, looked at him and grunted.

In the barn, in the deep straw, were the calves. They were black and white mostly, but there were a few brown ones called Jerseys. Edmond liked them best because they reminded him of his own soft brown jersey, although when they let him touch their soft faces, which they did sometimes, their faces felt different from the jersey. The calves did not say much, but they looked at Edmond with big wide-open eyes.

By the side of the house, in the nearby fields, were the cows, who came into the barn every evening to be milked, and then they went back again to their fields for the night. Edmond thought they must feel cold out there all night, but they never said anything to him about it. In their field lived the big old brown horse called Ned. He was retired and didn't leave the field very often. Edmond gave Ned sugar.

All around the farmhouse, on the track and between the barns, lived the hens – brown ones. There was one big cock which Edmond especially liked, although the cock stalked away from Edmond when he approached, crying out as he went. Some of the hens even went along the track as it went on downhill. If Edmond found them there he chased them back to the farm.

Down the track at the bottom of the hill was a copse with great tall trees in it. Mostly they were beech trees, and you could walk under them on hot days and it was beautifully cool. In the top of the trees lived the crows. They built big nests up there. When the crows saw Edmond, they flew out of their nests; they didn't come down to him, but they shouted excitedly. Except for going in the car (which didn't count) the copse was the furthest from home that Edmond had ever been.

Edmond goes away

One afternoon Edmond came out of the house and said to himself – he said it aloud, so that anyone could hear who wanted to – "I am going to walk far away." He stamped both his feet on the ground to see that his sandals were well and truly buckled. He banged his hands on his arms, to see that his arms would swing well. He kicked out his legs and jumped up and down a few times, to see his legs were in good shape for walking far away. Then he started off.

First, he went to the ducks. The ducks swam towards him. "Ducks," Edmond said, "I am going far away."

"Quack," said the ducks. "Quack-away."

Then Edmond went to the pigsty and said to the fat pig, "I am going far away."

"Oink," said the fat pig. "Oink-away."

Then Edmond went to the calves and said to them, "I am going far away."

But the calves said nothing, they just opened their eyes wider than ever and stared at Edmond.

So Edmond went to the gate of the cows' field and said to them, "I am going far away."

"Moo, moowar moo-way," said the cows, and Ned the old horse echoed them, singing out, "Neigh, neigh-away."

Then Edmond set off down the track towards the copse. Three or four hens popped out of the hedge as he set off and he stopped for a moment to chivvy them back towards the house.

"Tchuck-away, tchuck-away, tchuck-away," they said as they pattered up the path. Edmond strode on down the hill, hoping that his friends the crows would talk to him when he got to the copse.

They didn't let him down. They had seen him coming and he had barely got under the branches of the trees when they came swarming out of their nests, calling, "Cor, cor, cor," as they came.

Edmond put his head back and shouted up to them, "Crows, I am going far away – far away, crows."

And the crows heard him, and they called back, "Cor, cor, cor-away, cor-away." They circled round with a lot of excited flapping and then slowly, one by one, they settled back into the trees.

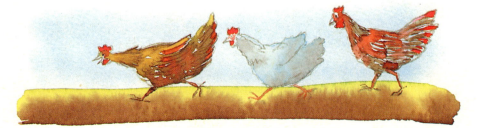

Edmond was in no hurry to leave the copse. He walked all round inside, patted several trees with his hands — the beech trees had nice, smooth bark and he stood by one small tree to see if he could get his arms all round it: he just could. Then it was time to go.

"Goodbye trees," Edmond whispered.

"Shsh, shsh," said the trees. "Shsh-away."

Beyond the copse, the path went on downhill a little way. At the bottom it was quite boggy and the path had some thick, green grass on it. There were deep tracks which were full of water, where the tractor had gone. Edmond got close to the fence and passed the marshy bit without getting his feet wet. Then he walked up the hill — on and on towards the top. He had seen the top of the hill many times, but he had never been there. Soon he would be over the top of the hill. Soon he would be far away.

The long march

The path up the hill, which Edmond had seen often from his bedroom window at home, had not looked very long, but it went on and on. As Edmond marched up it he began to wish he had someone with him. Then he thought to himself that perhaps he had some of his friends with him: he was leading a long line of them up the hill.

He thought that immediately behind him he would like to have old Ned the horse, because if he got tired he would be able to have a ride on him. Behind the horse he would have several of the crows. The crows would be very noisy, but as he got further and further away he could send the crows ahead to spy out the land. Cows, he thought, would be useful to have with him, because if he got thirsty he could have a drink of milk and if some hens rode on the back of the cows, perhaps one of them might give him an egg.

The calves wouldn't give him any milk, but when they got to the top of the hill they would be such good look-outs. He would stand four of them, one pointing in each direction, and they could tell him if anyone was coming. He couldn't think what the old pig would do, but he would like her to come. He thought she would probably want to bring twelve little piglets with her and she would be busy keeping them in order.

The three ducks would be good, because they made such a noise. Edmond himself had been quite frightened by their noise at first. If he met someone he didn't like, he would tell the ducks to quack at them and he was sure they would go away. Edmond made several loud quacks himself, not that there was anyone he could see at the moment, but the noise was satisfying. It made him feel that all his friends really were just behind him.

It occurred to Edmond that he could have people from inside his house to help him as well as all these outside friends. Ten of his red-coated soldiers would be handy if there were any enemies. Then, he could have his rocking horse in case old Ned got tired and wanted a rest. And, finally, he would have to have the black and white panda who shared his bed. Panda would come last in the line. He was very good at keeping away enemies.

Edmond kept marching on and on. He had been climbing steadily up the hill. Suddenly he realized he was very close to the top. His shadowy friends who had been following him all disappeared. He was Edmond, all alone and going far away. He threw up his arms in excitement and ran on to the top of the hill.

Edmond looked down on all the new country which he could claim as his own. Away to his left stretched great yellow fields of wheat, waiting to be harvested. To his right there was a village nestling among trees, and he could see the tall tower of a church and beyond, the land rose again and on the top of the hill there was something which looked suspiciously like a castle.

Best of all, right below him and not very far away, was

a lake. On one side, the lake ended in rushes and then there were trees. On the other, the lake had quite a steep bank and there was a boat tied up to it. On the lake there was a single swan swimming round and round, while among the rushes were green and brown ducks dabbling their beaks in the mud.

All this was Edmond's country. He wanted to hug it all. He had found it by going far away.

A night far away

Edmond had been so excited by the sight of his new country that he had run a few steps down the other side of the hill. Now he found he could no longer see the copse, his fields, the barn or the farmhouse. He ran quickly back onto the top of the hill, looked back the way he had come.

There was the farmhouse; he could see his bedroom window and just make out one of his yellow curtains which had been caught by the wind and was now lazily flapping in the breeze. Edmond turned the other way and looked at his new world; he was on a boundary between the Old World and the New. He hesitated for a moment, wondering which way to go. Then his eye caught a movement quite close to him. A familiar figure was walking up the path towards him. It was his father.

Edmond gave him a half wave and turned into the New World. He walked down to the lake where the rushes grew. The ground got very boggy but there were tussocks you could stand on safely. Edmond pulled at the reeds; they were firmly rooted but finally he got up a good long one which he held up in front of him like a sword as he walked on round the lake.

Where the boat was moored, Edmond found the bank was propped up by some wooden boards which had been driven into the water. This meant you could walk right up to the edge of the lake. Lying down, he could lean over the edge then just get his hand into the water and make some satisfactory waves which rocked the boat.

Edmond got up, pulled on the rope that moored the boat and, when it was against the bank, jumped in. In the boat were oars, but they were too big for Edmond to use although he could just lift them. Just then Edmond's father came up. He put down a big bundle he was carrying, untied the rope that moored the boat and stepping down into it pushed them out into the lake.

Edmond was surprised to see how well his father rowed. They rowed out to the centre of the lake because Edmond wished to speak to the swan. But the swan swam away from them in a circle. They rowed after it, but it kept circling. They tried to row straight towards it. It looked at them, but bowed its head twice at them, quite politely, and then swam away.

They moored the boat again and Edmond walked round the lake, picking up wood that had collected at the edge. In his bundle, Edmond's father had a frying pan and some sausages. They built a fire with the drift-wood and ate sausages, baked beans and filled up with bags of crisps.

By now it was quite dark and the moon had come up. Edmond was glad to find that his father had brought him his sleeping bag. They had built their fire a little up the hill from the lake. Edmond could snuggle down and look out over the water. Wreaths of mist spiralled up from the lake. They looked, Edmond thought, like ghostly people, but friendly because they came from his lake. As they grew bigger he saw that they had the faces of all the people he liked best. All the people he had left at home when he had come far away.

Edmond comes home

The bright sun shone into his eyes and Edmond woke up. A breeze was blowing the last of the mist off the lake. The swan was up and swimming round in endless circles again. Edmond's father was sitting propped against a rock, wrapped in a blanket. Edmond thought he might be asleep, but as soon as he moved, his father opened his eyes and smiled at him.

Edmond slid out of his sleeping bag, pulled on his sandals, stood up and looked around. The ducks remained in the reeds, but the swan came half out of the water and shook its wings as if it were going to fly off. In the end it settled back into the water and glided towards Edmond, bowing goodbye to him. Edmond noticed that there were some crows in the trees by the lake. Next time he would go and talk to them.

Edmond's father seemed inclined to stay asleep. Edmond put the frying pan back into the rucksack and bundled his sleeping bag beside it. He pointed up the hill and his father nodded, smiling at him but saying nothing. Edmond turned and waved goodbye to the swan and to the ducks who were just emerging from the reeds.

Edmond wondered if his home would look exactly the same when he got to the top of the hill: perhaps during the night the whole landscape had changed. Farm, barn, copse, crows, calves, cows, pig, horse and even ducks might have gone. Instead, there might be a huge town with great blocks of houses built in concrete. Edmond was in a hurry to get to the top of the hill.

He shut his eyes for the last three or four steps up the hill and shuffled forward. When he could feel he was on top of the hill, he took several deep breaths before he opened his eyes. It was still all there. The farm looked the same, although his bedroom window had been shut and the yellow curtain scooped back inside. The barn still stood solid and square. In the field by the house were the cows and Ned. Ned was still there, he had not been far away.

Edmond ran down to the copse. While he had been away the leaves seemed to have come out more. They were greener and brighter. He rushed in among them and ran up to the small tree. It had got smaller. He could get his arms round it much more easily. And where were the crows? He had come from the wrong way and they had not noticed him. He dashed out of the copse, shouting, "Crows, crows, I'm here." Now they heard him and came pouring out of their nests, swooping down towards him. "Crows!" Edmond shouted. "I have been far away."

"Cor-away," they cried.

As Edmond hurried up the track to the farm, the crows flew round in groups, calling again and again. This excited the hens who came bustling down the track to meet him. "Tchuck-away, tchuck-away," they clucked. The big cock was there, poking his head at Edmond. He let forth a loud cock-crow. Was it really Edmond come back?

The cows were clustered along the edge of the field, lowing at Edmond, "Moo-way, moo-way." Ned, the old horse, leaned over the gate, arching his neck and shaking his head with excitement. The calves said nothing, as usual, but they all lined the front of the open barn and stood there staring and staring at Edmond. And the pig? The old sow was no longer alone. She had at least twelve piglets with her. She actually stood up and came forward to grunt at Edmond and the piglets came squealing along beside her to gasp in amazement at this stranger. Edmond paused to try and count the piglets, but they ran about so much it was impossible. The ducks were all on their pond and paddled quickly over.

"Ducks," said Edmond, "I have been far away."

"Quack-away," they squawked back. Some came waddling out of their pond onto the grass to greet him.

Then he went over to stand at the front door of the house for a moment; to stand and stare at all his friends for a moment and look over towards the hill and know that behind it was another country. It was probably still there. He would look at it again soon.

"I have been far away!" he shouted as he turned to enter his home. "I have been far away, and I have come back."